When I Grow Up...

I want to be an Engineer

Written by Rhea Irvin
Edited by Breana Irvin
Illustrated by Fiverr

This book is dedicated to my parents, Willie and Peggy Murry,

who have always encouraged and inspired me

to reach for my dreams.

Love you both,

Rhea

When I grow up
I want to be

the best at what

I choose for me!

When I grow up

I want to be an

AEROSPACE ENGINEER...

who sends people to

infinity and beyond.

When I grow up

I want to be an

AUDIO ENGINEER...

who makes music

for all to hear.

When I grow up
I want to be a
CHEMICAL ENGINEER...
who makes skin care
and food that
helps us live.

When I grow up

I want to be a

COMPUTER ENGINEER...

who does web and

game designs for

all to enjoy throughout

the year.

When I grow up
I want to be an

ELECTRICAL ENGINEER...

who lights things

far and near.

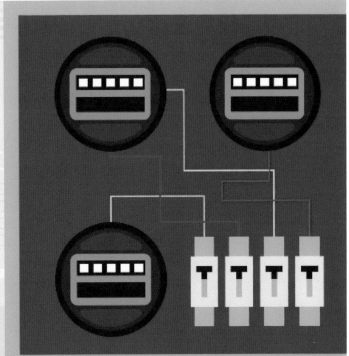

When I grow up

I want to be an

ENVIRONMENTAL

ENGINEER...

who makes our air and

water pure so we

can live.

When I grow up

I want to be a

PACKING ENGINEER...

Who designs and makes

packages for products

to survive in the

atmosphere.

When I grow up

I want to be a

PYROTECHNIC ENGINEER...

who lights up the night sky

with colorful displays

while people cheer.

When I grow up

I want to be a

ROBOTIC ENGINEER...

who makes automation

designs for task too

hard to bear.

What do you want to be...

Aerospace Engineer

Audio Engineer

Chemical Engineer

Computer Engineer

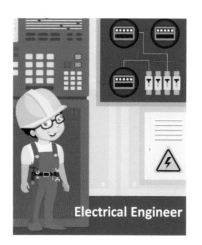

Electrical Engineer

Environmental Engineer

Packaging Engineer

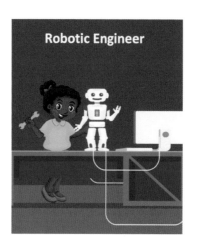

Robotic Engineer

Pyrotechnic Engineer

Engineering Careers Definitions

Aerospace Engineer- designs, develops and oversees the production of air and space vehicles.

Audio Engineer- designs, develops and produces audio/musical technology.

*****Biomedical Engineer**- analyzes and designs solutions that improve patient care.

Chemical Engineer- manipulates the interactions of individual atoms and molecules.

*****Ceramic Engineer**- creates objects from inorganic , non-metallic materials through technology.

*****Civil Engineer**- designs, constructs, and maintains physical and natural built environment and structure components of buildings.

Computer Engineer- develops and improves the software programs and hardware that make computers run.

Electrical Engineer- designs application of equipment, devices and systems which use electricity.

Environmental Engineer- creates solutions that will protect and improve the health of living organisms and the quality of the environment.

*****Fashion Engineer** – designs and manufactures textiles and fiber products as well as designs fashion machinery.

*****Forest Engineer**- works to ensure the health and sustainability of forestlands while allowing economic activities of timber harvest and recreational use to occur.

Engineering Careers Definitions

Geological Engineer- analyzes and recommends designs associated with essentials in the area of earth-structure interactions.

Marine Engineer- develops and designs operation maintenance of ocean technology.

Packing Engineer- designs, evaluates and produces products for distribution through packaging.

Plastic Engineer- designs, develops and manufactures plastic for products.

Preservation Engineer- evaluates historical buildings, consults on renovations and ensures cost-effectiveness of projects.

Pyrotechnic Engineer- experiments with materials and combinations to create productions that will enhance the performance of firework displays and fire related special effects in movies/television.

Sports Engineer- researches and develops equipment and environment of the sports industry, from shoes to stadiums/arenas.

Systems Engineer- designs and manages complex systems core over their lifecycle.

Robotic Engineer- designs, builds and test robots and flexible automation that are productive and safe to operate and maintain.

*Not illustrated in the book

Printed in Poland
by Amazon Fulfillment
Poland Sp. z o.o., Wrocław